Littlest Pet Shop™

SUPERSTYLISH PETS

ACTIVITY BOOK
WITH STICKERS

by Alison Inches
illustrated by Jim Talbot

SCHOLASTIC INC.

New York   Toronto   London   Auckland   Sydney
Mexico City   New Delhi   Hong Kong   Buenos Aires

ISBN-13: 978-0-439-88785-4
ISBN-10: 0-439-88785-2

12 11 10 9 8 7 6 5   7 8 9 10 11/0

Printed in the U.S.A.
First printing, January 2007

PET BIRTHDAYS

There's nothing a Littlest Pet Shop pet loves more than a birthday, and the month your pet was adopted says a lot about its personality. Of course, the same thing goes for your birthday month—it says a lot about you! Check out this chart to learn more about yourself *and* about your favorite littlest pets.

January

Bling birthstone: Garnet

BEST COLOR: White

Fashion flower: Carnation

Star quality: January pets love to help others.

February

Bling birthstone: Amethyst

BEST COLOR: Dark blue

Fashion flower: Violet

Star quality: February pets are loyal to their families.

March

Bling birthstone: Aquamarine

BEST COLOR: Silver

Fashion flower: Daffodil

Star quality: March pets are very creative.

April

Bling birthstone: Diamond

BEST COLOR: Yellow

Fashion flower: Sweet pea

Star quality: April pets love competition.

May

Bling birthstone: Emerald

BEST COLOR: Lavender

Fashion flower: Lily of the valley

Star quality: May pets love beautiful things.

June

Bling birthstone: Alexandrite

BEST COLOR: Pink

Fashion flower: Rose

Star quality: June pets like to have fun.

July

Bling birthstone: Ruby

BEST COLOR: Sky blue

Fashion flower: Larkspur

Star quality: July pets enjoy time at home.

August

Bling birthstone: Peridot

BEST COLOR: Dark green

Fashion flower: Gladiolus

Star quality: August pets like to take chances.

September

Bling birthstone: Sapphire

BEST COLOR: Gold

Fashion flower: Aster

Star quality: September pets are caring and thoughtful.

October

Bling birthstone: Zirconium

BEST COLOR: Brown

Fashion flower: Marigold

Star quality: October pets would do anything for a friend.

November

Bling birthstone: Topaz

BEST COLOR: Purple

Fashion flower: Chrysanthemum

Star quality: November pets never give up.

December

Bling birthstone: Blue zircon

BEST COLOR: Red

Fashion flower: Narcissus

Star quality: December pets are adventurous.

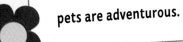

MAZE CRAZE

Can you help this little pet find his way through the maze to his best friend?

START

FINISH

WORD ACCESSORY SCRAMBLE

Unscramble each of the clue words.
The circled letters will spell out the adjective that best describes your favorite pet.

AATIR   ◯ __ __ __ __

CSRFA   __ __ __ ◯ __

RTEERTBA   __ __ __ __ __ ◯ __ __

SESUSNGSLA   __ __ __ ◯ __ __ __ __ __ __

AGNAHDB   __ __ __ __ ◯ __ __

RLYWEJE   __ __ __ __ __ __ ◯

Your favorite pet is. . .

__ __ __ __ __ __ __ __

What's Cookin' at the Doggie Diner?

Today's Menu:
* Animal Crisps
* Paws-atively Fruity Kabobs
* Purr-fect Trail Mix

Animal Crisps

Here's what you'll need:
* 3 large flour tortillas
* olive oil
* salt
* animal-shaped cookie cutters
* cookie sheet

Here's what you do:
1. First ask an adult for permission and for help using the oven.
2. Using the cookie cutters, cut shapes from the flour tortillas.
3. Arrange the animals on a cookie sheet.
4. Brush olive oil on each of the animals.
5. Sprinkle with salt.
6. Bake at 350° Fahrenheit for 7 minutes.
7. Eat them plain or dip them in salsa, guacamole, or hummus. Yum!

Paws-atively Fruity Kabobs

Here's what you'll need:

* ❋ 1 apple (peeled, seeded, and cut into small chunks)
* ❋ 6 large marshmallows
* ❋ peanut butter
* ❋ 1 sliced banana (sliced into circles)
* ❋ 2 wooden skewers

Here's what you do:

1. First ask an adult for permission.
2. Push a wooden skewer through a piece of apple, a marshmallow, and a piece of banana. Repeat two more times.
3. Spread peanut butter on one side of the kabob. Makes two kabobs.

Purr-fect Trail Mix

Here's what you'll need:

* ❋ 1 cup dried bananas
* ❋ 1 cup dried pineapple
* ❋ ½ cup almonds
* ❋ ½ cup shredded coconut
* ❋ ¼ cup mini chocolate chips

Here's what you do:

Combine ingredients and munch away!

SNACK ATTACK!

Pets love their treats, and there's nothing better than sharing a snack with a friend! What are your favorite foods? List them here.

Yummy Breakfasts

1. _____   3. _____

2. _____   4. _____

Luscious Lunches

1. _____
2. _____
3. _____
4. _____

Super Snacks

1. _____
2. _____
3. _____
4. _____

Delicious Dinners

1. _____
2. _____
3. _____
4. _____

DREAMY DESSERTS

1. _____
2. _____
3. _____
4. _____

PET PEEVE WORD SEARCH

Every pet has something that really bugs him.
Can you find the pet peeves listed below?
The words may read forward, backward, or diagonally.

cat fights

heights

DROOLING

losing

frizzy fur

noise

hairballs

rainy days

```
R T A T A N F G H S
L A G V B O N X A T
O L I M T I B G I H
S O X N L S T G R G
I B T O Y E U R B I
N R O I W D Y U A F
G R J K Q S A W L T
D L G E O G E Y L A
H E I G H T S T S C
F R I Z Z Y F U R U
```

Do you have any pet peeves? **WHAT BUGS YOU?**
Let it all hang out!

_____

_____

_____

TOTALLY TWINS!

Take a look at the picture on the left. Then look at the picture on the right.
Can you spot ten differences in these pictures? Find and circle them!

PICTURE PERFECT

Draw a picture of you and your favorite Littlest Pet Shop pet. Then use some of the stickers to decorate the page.

Pet Motto

What's the golden rule when it comes to your pets? Use the code below to figure it out!

☀ = K   ♥ = B
★ = P   ☮ = N
🌈 = D   ❀ = E
🌙 = O   🍦 = T
🦴 = Y   ☺ = U
🧯 = I   🎁 = S
🧁 = R

B E K I N D
T O Y O U R
P E T S .

PAMPERED PET WORD SEARCH

Every pet deserves to be pampered. Can you find the salon terms listed below?
The words may read forward or backward.

BARRETTES

BATH

BLOW-DRY

CLIPS

COMBS

CONDITIONER

HAIRCUT

HEADBAND

MANICURE

MASSAGE

NAIL POLISH

PEDICURE

RIBBON

SCRUNCHIES

SHAMPOO

UPDO

```
P U S E I H C N U R C S
E S H A I R C U T H R P
D E A T N F H G A S I I
I T M A S S A G E I B L
C T P D A D T O S L B C
U E O R T E S R A O O S
R R O N C O M B S P N B
E R A L R E A T I L G A
M A N I C U R E N I R T
M B I B D N A B D A E H
A C O N D I T I O N E R
B L O W D R Y A O D P U
```

Purr-fect Party Planner

Every little pet loves a good party! Use these pages to plan a party of your own. Make an invitation list, plan an amazing menu, and think of some fabulous party favors. Then come up with some dazzling decorating ideas and a few awesome party outfits.

I would *serve* these foods...

Appetizer:_____

Main course:_____

Snack food:_____

Drinks:_____

Dessert:_____

If I had a party, I would *invite*...

_____
_____
_____
_____
_____
_____
_____
_____
_____
_____
_____
_____
_____

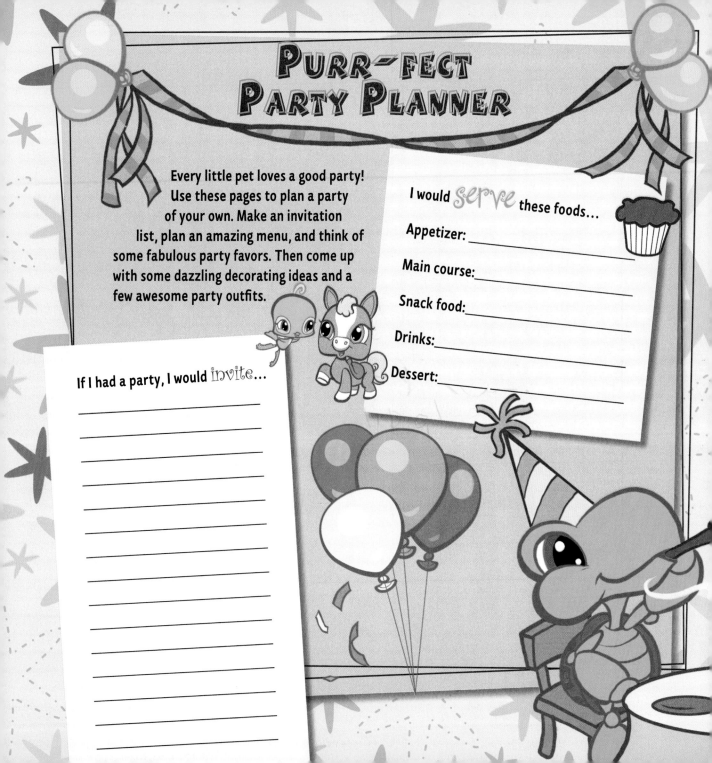

The dazzling *decorations* would be…

_____

_____

_____

_____

My fabulous *party favors* would include…

_____

_____

_____

_____

_____

My top five most awesome *party outfits* are…

1. _____

2. _____

3. _____

4. _____

5. _____

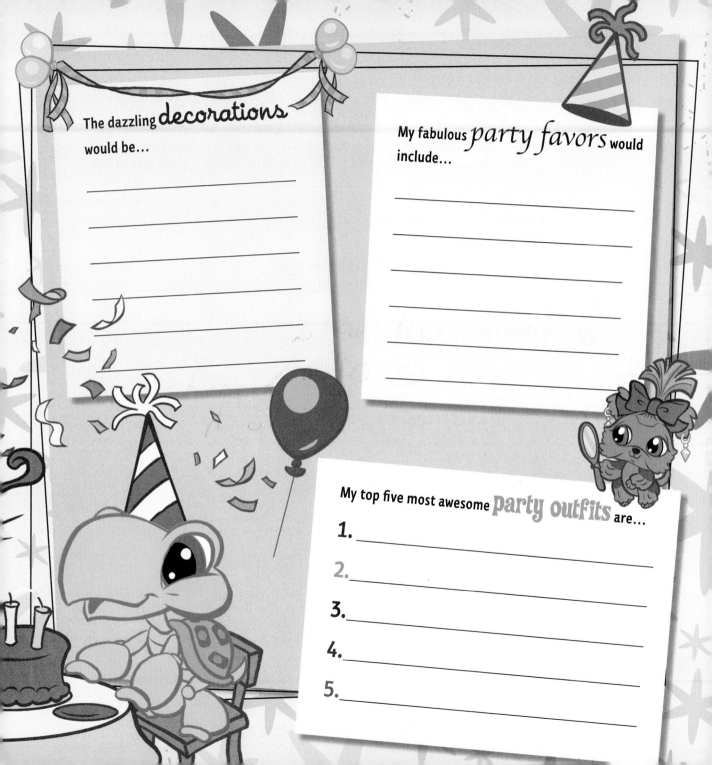

PERSONALITY PROFILES

There's nothing a pet loves more than her friends. And good friends always have things in common and some differences, too. Fill in these personality profiles. Then compare them to see how you and your friend are alike and how you're different. You can also tape or glue in a photo of you and your friend together if you have one. If not, draw a picture of the two of you together!

All About Me

My name is: _Gabriela_

My nickname is: _Gabby \ God_

My favorite accessory is: _lip glosh_

I like to: _tea_

I dislike: _____

My favorite food is: _____

I often say: _____

My deepest wish is: _____

All About My Friend

My friend's name is: _____

My friend's nickname is: _____

My friend's favorite accessory is: _____

My friend likes to: _____

My friend dislikes: _____

My friend's favorite food is: _____

My friend often says: _____ _____

My friend's deepest wish is: _____

_____

my friends

ANSWERS

Page 6

Page 15

Page 7

Tiara
Scarf
Barrette
Sunglasses
Handbag
Jewelry

TRENDY

Page 17

BE KIND TO YOUR PETS.

Page 19

P U S E I H C N U R C S
E S H A I R C U T H R P
D I E A T N F H G A S I I
I T T M A S S A G E I B L
C U P D A D T O S L O C
U R O R T E S R A O N S
R E A N C O M B S P O B
E R A L R E A T I L G A
M A N I C U R E N I R T
M B I B D N A B D A E H
A C O N D I T I O N E R
B L O W D R Y A O D P U

Page 13

R T A T A N F G H S
L A G V B O N X A I T
O L I M T I B G I R H
S O X N L S T G R B G
I B T O Y E U R U I I
N R O I W D Y U A F
G R J K Q S A W L T
D L G E O G E Y L A
H E I G H T S T S C
F R I Z Z Y F U R U